Disney · PIXAR

Cars

The Fast Lane

Adapted by Cynthia Hands
Illustrated by the Disney Storybook Artists
Designed by Disney Publishing's Global Design Group
Inspired by the art and character designs created by Pixar Animation Studios

A GOLDEN BOOK • NEW YORK

Copyright © 2006 Disney Enterprises, Inc./Pixar. Disney/Pixar elements © Disney/Pixar; Dodge is a trademark of DaimlerChrysler; Hudson Hornet is a trademark of DaimlerChrysler; Volkswagen trademarks, design patents and copyrights are used with the approval of the owner, Volkswagen AG; Fiat is a trademark of Fiat S.p.A.; Mack is a registered trademark of Mack Trucks, Inc.; Kenworth is a trademark of Paccar, Inc.; Chevrolet Impala is a trademark of General Motors; Porsche is a trademark of Porsche; Jeep is a registered trademark of DaimlerChrysler; Mercury is a registered trademark of Ford Motor Company; Plymouth Superbird is a trademark of DaimlerChrysler; Cadillac Coup de Ville is a trademark of General Motors. Sarge's rank insignia design used with the approval of the U.S. Army. Petty marks used by permission of Petty Marketing LLC. Inspired by the Cadillac Ranch by Ant Farm (Lord, Michels and Marquez) © 1974. All rights reserved. Published in the United States by Golden Books, an imprint of Random House Children's Books, a division of Random House, Inc., New York, and in Canada by Random House of Canada Limited, Toronto, in conjunction with Disney Enterprises, Inc. Golden Books, A Golden Book, and the G colophon are registered trademarks of Random House, Inc.

ISBN: 978-0-375-83377-9

www.randomhouse.com/kids/disney

Printed in the United States of America

24 23 22 21 20 19

The Dinoco 400 is about to begin. It's the biggest race
of the year . . .

. . . and Lightning McQueen wants to be the first rookie
to win the Piston Cup.

McQueen's pit crew wants to give him new tires,
but McQueen doesn't listen. He works alone.

With one lap to go, McQueen can taste victory,
until—*POP!*—his tires blow!

McQueen, The King, and Chick cross the finish line
at the same time! It's too close to call!

Chick and The King hear the news.
The tiebreaker race is one week away!

Almost winning is not good enough for McQueen.
He is not very proud of himself.

McQueen is scared! He gets lost and speeds into the quiet town of Radiator Springs—where he is chased by Sheriff.

"Take cover!" cries Sarge, the owner of the local supply shop.
He hasn't seen this much action in Radiator Springs in a long time!

It doesn't take long for McQueen to get into more trouble. As he races away from Sheriff, he gets tangled with the statue of the town's founder and wrecks the road.

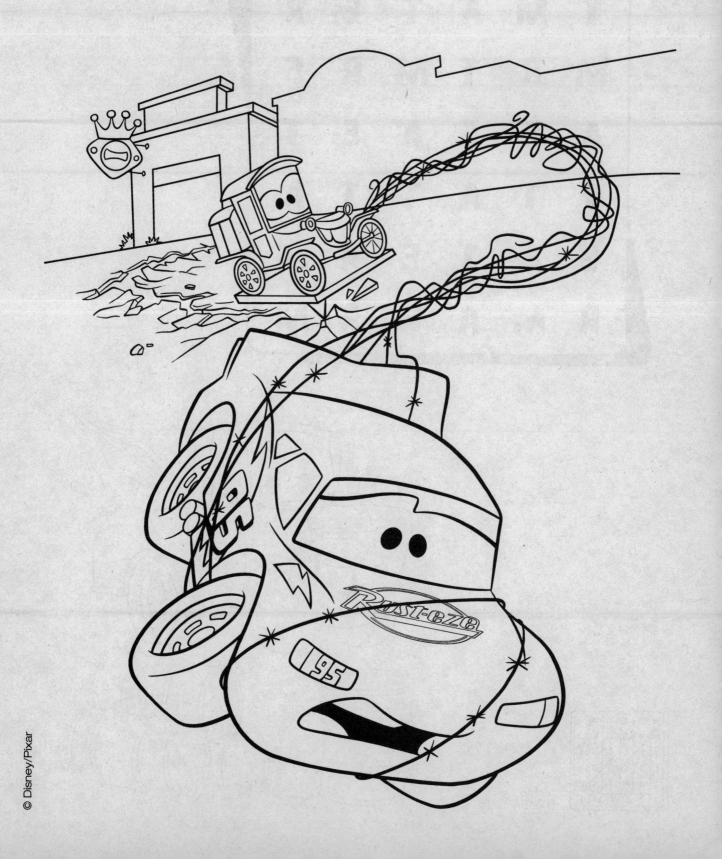

Mater is a tow truck in town. He likes to make new friends.
How many times can you find the name MATER in the puzzle?
Look up, down, forward, backward, and diagonally.

T	M	A	T	E	R
M	R	T	M	R	E
A	E	E	A	E	T
T	T	A	T	T	A
E	A	T	E	A	M
R	R	M	A	R	R	M

ANSWER: 6.

McQueen gets put into the car jail. He tries to trick Mater into letting him out.

When Sheriff shows up, he tells Mater to tow McQueen to court.

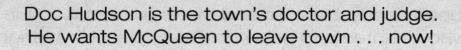

Doc Hudson is the town's doctor and judge.
He wants McQueen to leave town . . . now!

McQueen needs a lawyer, and Mater is the only car in town
who volunteers to help him. Everyone else is angry
with McQueen for ruining the main road.

Sally, the motel owner, comes to court and says that McQueen needs to fix the road he wrecked.

Doc tells McQueen that he has to fix the road with Bessie before he can leave town. Use the code to find out what Bessie is.

Doc says it will take five days to finish the road. McQueen is not happy. How will he get to the tiebreaker race now?

The first chance he gets, McQueen tries to leave town, but he doesn't make it very far. He runs out of gas! Sheriff took out his gas while he was sleeping.

As McQueen works on the road, everyone comes out to watch.
Flo owns the café where the townsfolk go
for the freshest oil and fuel.

Luigi owns the local tire shop.

Guido works at the tire shop with Luigi.
He can change a tire faster than anyone.

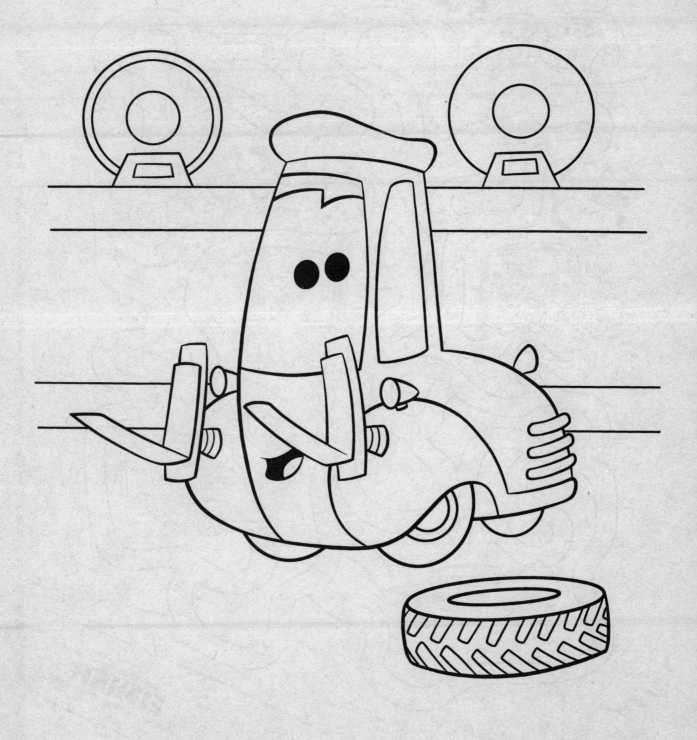

One day, the townsfolk get excited. Visitors arrive in town!
All the townsfolk try to sell them something from their shops, but
the visitors are just lost and want to find the Interstate. Help Mr. and
Mrs. Mini Van get through Radiator Springs without buying anything.

START

FINISH

ANSWER:

McQueen finishes the road in one hour! He does a very bad job.
Doc is angry. "Why don't we have a little race?" says Doc.
"Me and you." The loser will have to repave the road!

Just outside town, the two cars race in the dirt.
Much to his surprise, McQueen loses!

The next morning, Sally and Mater wake up to find a beautiful new stretch of road. McQueen worked all through the night. But where is he?

Doc finds McQueen on the dirt road where they raced. Doc tries to give McQueen a tip on how to race on dirt, but McQueen still can't make it to the finish line. What does Doc know that McQueen needs to learn? To find out, replace each letter below with the one that comes before it in the alphabet.

UVSO SJHIU UP HP MFGU

_ _ _ _   _ _ _ _ _   _ _   _ _   _ _ _ _ .

ANSWER: Turn right to go left.

Disney/Pixar elements © Disney/Pixar, not including underlying vehicles owned by third parties; Hudson Hornet™

Back in town, Guido and Luigi want to sell McQueen new tires,
but he is still grumpy about not being able to race on dirt.

Mater wants to show McQueen how to have some real fun.
He teaches McQueen to tip tractors!

What does Mater have that help him drive backward?
(Hint: McQueen does not have them.)
Follow the lines from the letters to the boxes to find out.

V E E W A R R I   R R M O I S R

ANSWER: Rearview mirrors.

Later that night, to thank him for doing a good job on the road,
Sally lets McQueen stay at her motel.

The next day, McQueen finds three Piston Cups
in Doc's back office. Doc is a racing legend!

"You're the Fabulous Hudson Hornet!" says a surprised McQueen. But Doc is angry at McQueen, because Doc has always kept this a secret from the townsfolk.

Detailed to perfection! Radiator Springs looks good on McQueen.
Ka-chow!

After the race, McQueen decides to make Radiator Springs
his new home . . . and Sally wants to be the first
to help him practice his racing skills.

McQueen has learned how important true friends are. He even keeps a promise by getting Mater a ride in the Dinoco helicopter. Find 5 things that are different in the bottom picture.

After seeing what a good guy McQueen is,
Dinoco wants to sponsor the rookie, but McQueen
is staying with his friends at Rust-eze.

Chick gets the Piston Cup, but no one cares.
The fans are sick of his dirty tricks.

Thanks to McQueen, The King finishes his very last race!

Chick ends up winning the big race,
but McQueen is the *real* winner.

Seeing The King crash makes McQueen think about what
happened to Doc. He decides to do the right thing
and gives up the Piston Cup to help The King.

Chick will do anything not to come in behind The King.
He makes The King crash!

Heading into the final lap of the race,
Chick bumps into McQueen again. McQueen remembers
Doc's advice, "Turn right to go left," and he gets back in the lead.

McQueen is ready to race again!
Look up, down, forward, backward, and diagonally to find the names of the friends who helped McQueen get back in the race.

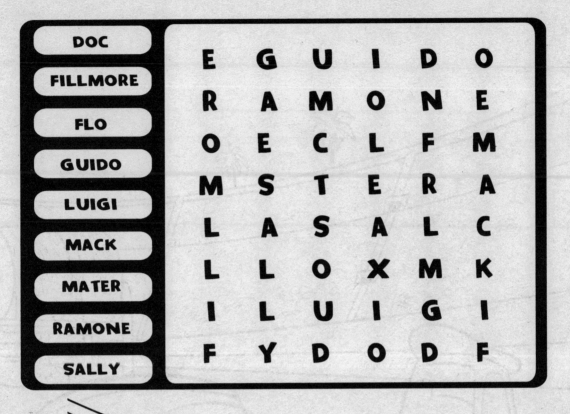

Word List:
- DOC
- FILLMORE
- FLO
- GUIDO
- LUIGI
- MACK
- MATER
- RAMONE
- SALLY

Puzzle Grid:

E	G	U	I	D	O
R	A	M	O	N	E
O	E	C	L	F	M
M	S	T	E	R	A
L	A	S	A	L	C
L	L	O	X	M	K
I	L	U	I	G	I
F	Y	D	O	D	F

ANSWER:

© Disney/Pixar

McQueen arrives at the pit, and Guido changes all four
of his tires in record time!

Using one of his dirty tricks, Chick brushes against McQueen,
causing McQueen to get a flat tire.
McQueen radios Doc, his new crew chief, for help.

Lightning McQueen feels ready to race now that he knows his friends are there to help. *Ka-chow!* Watch out, Chick!

McQueen gets a big surprise when Doc shows up
with some other Radiator Springs friends to help him.

The King is going strong in his last-ever race,
with Chick close behind him.

As hard as it is for McQueen, he leaves town for the big race. But once he's there, he can't stop thinking about all his friends back in Radiator Springs.

Suddenly, reporters looking for McQueen arrive.
They ask lots of questions about why he's been hiding in the
small town when the big race is only a few days away!

McQueen wants to cruise with Sally, too.
Radiator Springs seems more like home to him now.

McQueen looks great! Now Sally wants to cruise with the race car who helped change her town.

That night, McQueen finishes paving the road. Now it's time for him to go shopping. Radiator Springs finally has a customer! He will start with new tires from Luigi and some bumper stickers from Lizzie.